Rhymes & Ramblings of a
Small Town Girl

Judy Bruns

COCO PUBLICATIONS
COLDWATER, OH

Published in 2019, by Coco Publications

Coldwater, OH 45828

Bruns, Judy

Rhymes & Ramblings of a Small Town Girl

Story by Judy Bruns / Illustrations by Andrea Bruns

ISBN

0-9713926-3-3

Library of Congress Control Number

2019906426

Edited by Judy Bruns Book Design by Andrea Bruns

PRINTED IN THE UNITED STATES OF AMERICA

DEDICATION:

To family and friends, with love. . .
I am blessed and thankful.

Table of Contents

Small Town. . . Beginnings

Prenatal 3

Twins 4

From the Solace of the Womb 5

Small Town. . . Childhood

Mama Couldn't Carry a Tune 9

My Little Blue Pedal Car 10

Childhood Hideaways 11

Kids & Skates & No More Rain 13

My, What a Time at the Denneys'! 15

Sent to the Corner AGAIN! 16

Tammy 18

Freckle Cream! 20

A Babysitter's Nightmare! 23

If I Could Only Revisit That Time 25

Small Town. . . Gifts of Nature

A Single Firefly 29

Butterfly 30

Stubby-tailed Squirrel 31

The Rain Inside 33

There's a Sparrow Out Back 34

Dandelions 35

Acrobat Squirrel 36

TABLE OF CONTENTS CONTINUED...

Small Town. . . Gifts of Nature Cont...

Summer Rain 37

Ant Hill 38

Maydrops 39

Small Town. . . Family Life

What's in a Name? 43

What's in the Glass? 44

A Prestigious Golf Award 45

Finding Time 47

What's That, Cat? 48

The Haircut 49

Wisecracks in the Kitchen 51

Good Intentions 52

Her First Car (The "Orange Bomber") 53

Grandma's Park 54

Watching Jackie Run! 55

Grandma's Reclining Reading Chair 56

Our Dog Barney and the Pesky Fly 57

Deck of Cards 58

Goodbye, Good Friend 59

Yuck! The Candy Didn't Taste Good! 61

You Bring Me Patience 62

TABLE OF CONTENTS CONTINUED...

Small Town. . . Teacher Tales

"Mrs. Tinkler" 65

Follow the Bouncing Eyeball 66

My Contribution to Science 67

What We Do with What We've Got 68

Be Careful What You Reveal 70

Animal Bribery in the Classroom 71

Please Lead 72

The Object of Envy 73

L.A. Rap 74

Small Town. . . Life Lessons Along the Way

One Ford Taurus vs. One Crossing Doe . .77

Nick's Joy 78

Precious Child 79

Rising Above the Pain with Humility . .80

Medals on the Wall 81

I'd Make a Poor Hunter 82

It Could Have Been Me 83

On the Rebound 84

Give Us This Day 85

TABLE OF CONTENTS CONTINUED...

Small Town. . . Past "50"

Who Stole My Face? 89

Transformation (Middle-age Spread and Other Alarming Features) 90

Sleepless Nights (Aging Hormones Meet Writer's Block) 91

Lighten Up! 92

After "59" 93

Small Town. . . Retirement

Abby's Pretty Toenails 97

A Boat Afloat After Winter 98

Along My Morning Path 99

Our A.D. Dixie Dog 100

Small Town. . . Profound

Her Contribution to a Candidate 105

Untitled 106

She Died on Her Birthday 107

Seeing Haiti from on Top 108

Lunch with Aunt Alvira 109

The Sea Gull 112

At the Nursing Home 113

TABLE OF CONTENTS CONTINUED...

Small Town. . . Faith

This Earthly Life 117

Needle in a Haystack? (How About a Contact Lens in a Lawn?) 118

When You Thought No One Was Watching (. . .He Was.) 119

The Most Glorious Sight (Revelation— at the Gas Pump) 120

Putting God in Line 121

Showing Respects 122

The Big Picture 123

Awaken My Senses 124

My pen compensates

For heartfelt melodies

My throat cannot utter.

I sing in my poems.

~ Judy Bruns

Small Town...

Beginnings

Prenatal

Curled in soft, warm water;
Relaxed, peaceful;
Mother's voice a lullaby
That soothes me
Cradles me
Back to sleep
Inside my first home.

TWINS

Rambunctious little siblings

Swimming inside their mom—

"I feel them kick!" she says with glee

While the twins have barrels of fun.

They "tag" each other back and forth;

Then up and down they go.

It's better than a trampoline;

They're stars of a picture show!

Doc tells their mom, "It won't be long,

They'll start to run out of room."

"I'm ready for this!" their mother replies.

"Today would be none too soon!"

As for the twins, they're both content

To grow a little bit more,

And if you think they're spunky now,

Just wait till after they're born!

FROM THE SOLACE OF THE WOMB

From the solace of the womb,

With the tempo of a heartbeat for a song,

The child once enveloped in a cushion of warmth

Now emerges to nestle in a mother's arms.

Small Town...
Childhood

Mama Couldn't Carry a Tune

Mama couldn't carry a tune

In that creaking rocking chair,

But she'd hum away my monsters

Till they vanished in the air.

I'd climb on her lap, curl in her arms,

Then wait as the monsters scattered.

With Mama humming, sweet but off-key,

It was her love, not her notes, that mattered.

MY LITTLE BLUE PEDAL CAR

There was nothing so grand when I was 3-years-old as cruising down the sidewalk in my little blue pedal car, a sleek convertible with white trim and silver bumpers. Sitting behind that steering wheel, I felt like the coolest kid in town.

One unforgettable day when I was busy collecting envious "oohs" and "ahhs" from the neighbor kids, Mom's melodious voice rang out in its usual happy tone, "Sup—per!" I heard her clearly enough, but I was quite content in my magnificent automobile. As I passed under tall tree branches alive with birds and squirrels, I just knew they, too, were chattering about my car, and I loved all the attention it was getting.

A while later, my mother's voice was not so pleasant. "Judy! Come in for supper!" Surely she understood my delay, I thought. I was in the middle of something very important. Now, a couple little kids across the street were tugging on their parents' sleeves asking for permission to walk over to see my car. I couldn't disappoint them. I pedaled with pride.

"Judy! Did you hear your mother call you for supper? Get in the house NOW!" Uh oh! The words that filled the air this time were deeper, serious, and were coming my way fast. I tried to get out of my pedal car, but my arms and legs froze. I looked up to find myself staring into the face of my dad! I couldn't remember him being so tall before. I was in trouble!

With one scoop of his hand, my father lifted me up and out of my little blue car. And with three swishes of his other hand, he swatted my rear end in front of all my admirers. I can still feel the flush of embarrassment on my face—and the heat of a spanking on my behind—after all these years. I imagine my cheeks, both sets, were a bit rosy. Dad carried me and my pedal car home. I was wrapped in his one arm, and my pedal car was dragging from his other.

I don't remember what we had for supper. What stands out in my mind is that my father demanded my obedience that day, and he got it. He also demanded my respect. He got that, too. While my parents had often let me know that they loved me, I was being prepared for a world where there are rules to follow and expectations to meet.

Sometimes we just have to learn the hard way.

Childhood Hideaways

Everyone needs their own private place where they can get away from the rest of the world, to think, to imagine and—as a child—to hide and to play.

I first developed hiding places as a game when I was 3 years old. I would hide in the hallway clothes hamper, and when my mother opened the lid, I'd jump up like a jack-in-the-box to surprise her! Sometimes I was the one who got the first surprise—a face full of dirty laundry!

Then there were days I would scrunch up into a ball and hide beneath the kitchen sink as Mother cleared the table, preparing to wash the dishes only inches from my head and my knees. I listened to the water running and squishing around above me, and to the gulping suction of the pipes when the emptied dishwater came past my ears down the drain. Then, before Mom could move away from the sink, Voila! I pushed open the cupboard door, and out popped her little girl!

When I grew past the stage of hiding in clothes hampers and underneath sinks, I tried out the dog house in our back yard. It had been built much too big for Spooky, our fox terrier, anyway. However, he didn't appreciate the intrusion, and I didn't appreciate stepping into the doo-doo in his dog house yard. That particular hideaway didn't last too long, needless to say.

When Mom hung out bed linens on the clothesline to dry, I remember how I wrapped myself in the fresh, clean smell of the sheets. I was convinced that as I stood in their folds, I was invisible to the world—until my mother walked over to the two bare feet showing on the dewy grass, beneath the hanging sheets. She patted me on the behind and grinned like she had just discovered her own ornery little elf.

As I grew a bit older, the cemetery next to our house became the perfect place for me to hide, during the daytime, that is! It amazed me that no one else had taken advantage of its refuge. Many a day I torpedoed through the line of bushes that separated our property from the cemetery, to crouch behind a tombstone as my mother called out, "Judy! Where are you? You need to come in and clean up your

room!" Sometimes my determination kept me concealed for an hour or more until I finally tired of the game. Reluctantly, yet feeling a sense of victory, too, I slid out from my hiding place to do my chores.

In later years, I would sit with a paper tablet beneath the broad, tall trees of that cemetery to write and draw. Surrounded by chirping birds, scampering squirrels, and an occasional bunny or two, it became my favorite, peaceful, beautiful hiding place of all. I miss it. Somehow, my home office "hide-away," though it has a window view of backyard nature, isn't quite the same as sitting at the base of a big, old tree.

KIDS & SKATES & NO MORE RAIN

Rain draws lines down our storm door window, and holes become puddles on the street. Sparrows huddle for safety deep in the branches of our two maples. I huddle, too—inside the house, on the floor, looking out of the glass panels, hoping the sun will finally shine again.

It's not fair! At least the neighbor kids have brothers and sisters to play with inside on days like this, but I'm left with no one. It's not fun being an only child. It's not fun being alone.

At least I have my dog. "Here, Spooky. Come here, fella. Crawl up on my lap. What would I do without you? You love it when I scratch your head, don't you, buddy?

"Hey! Spooky! Come back here! I'm more important than chasing a big old fly, ain't I? Okay, just be that way. Go runnin' off and let me alone again."

I wonder how long the rain will last. Mom's in the basement doing laundry. Why on a day like this? Does she know something I don't? It's hard to get her attention when she's working, so I might as well not even try. Besides, moms don't understand what it's like to be an eight-year-old kid anyway.

The clouds seem to be spreading apart. But maybe it's my imagination. If I sit here cross-legged in front of this door window—and cross my fingers—long enough, though, maybe the rain will stop. Diane, Mikey, Beth, and I will be able to get out our skates again. Mine fit great over my saddle shoes, and they don't slip out when I go down the sidewalk hill next door.

Okay, maybe if I sit cross-legged, cross my fingers, and hold my breath for ten seconds, the rain will stop. . .

What if I do it fifteen seconds?. . .

Where did I put that four-leaf clover from Mrs. Heuker's front yard? If I wish on that, sit cross-legged, cross my fingers, and hold my breath for twenty seconds, that ought to do the trick.

Okay, this is boring. I'm getting tired. . . Z-Z-Z-Z -- Z-Z-Z

"Judy! Judy! What are you doing sleeping by the front door? Why aren't you outside playing with the neighbor kids? Diane just called and wants to sidewalk skate."

Yeah! It worked! The sun is shining! Birds are out of hiding; they're pulling worms out of the wet grass. I hear cars splashing through puddles and neighbor kids shouting from two doors down! Where are my saddle shoes? Where are my roller skates? No more rain!

My What a Time at the Denneys'!

Maurice made a swing set
For the kids in the whole neighborhood!
He spared no parts, no time nor skill;
High and sturdy it stood!

He made two swings for soaring,
A trapeze to hang by our heels,
And some rings for us to monkey on
Where we'd dangle, laugh, and squeal!

Maurice made all kinds of things
For his kids and those on our street,
From Tarzan ropes and tree lofts,
To stilts fit for little feet.

When neighbor kids weren't busy
Playing tag or playing ball,
We were likely at the Denneys',
The favorite yard of us all.

Sent to the Corner AGAIN!

Towering above the class, yardstick in hand, Mrs. "V" klop-klop-klops her way to my desk with familiarity. I look up to see a stern and narrow brow, framed in gray, leaning over my head. Avoiding the inevitable, I drop my gaze to the floor. There I am again confronted, this time by her thick-heeled, black tie-shoes, planted solidly side-by-side next to my seat.

I risk a glance upward. Bifocaled eyeballs meet my own eyes, and I lower my head once more in defeat. When will I ever learn? The class "jabber box" has been nabbed in the act again—this time verbalizing with pal, Linda Z. Though I know I shouldn't whisper in Mrs. "V's" room (It's a sin, isn't it?), I just CAN'T suppress the urge to talk.

"Quiet!" The order blasts into my ears and bounces off all four walls before the impact finally subsides. I see venom spilling from the sides of my teacher's mouth. "Corner!" Her skill with one-word commands has sharpened with practice, most which she's acquired through me.

My face flushes; my freckles take on a shade of florescent green. (Why was I born a fair-skinned redhead?) Class members point at the human chameleon in row three—me— as they rollick with loud guffaws. With resignation, I slowly rise from my seat, head barely peeking above my shoulders, to find my spot in the northwest corner of the room.

A line of windows borders my left, and a blackboard hangs from the wall on my right. Out of the corner of my eye, from beneath a smudged, half-drawn window shade, I see 1st grade children frolicking on the playground below our 2nd floor classroom. *Ah, freedom. . .* I daydream. I picture myself running headlong into the double-loop jump rope to the rhythm of "Teddy Bear, Teddy Bear, turn around. Teddy Bear, Teddy Bear, touch the ground," and then I imagine being named the new, evasive 2nd grade champ at dodge ball. I would be there on the playground; I would even be at home, sick in bed, or ANYwhere but here, where I stand confined. I wish carefree kids on playgrounds throughout the whole world could understand the magnitude of my pain and the depth of my despair. While they bask in their fun and freedom, another stands as in jail, face drawn, nose pressed forever into a right angle, a prisoner to her own congeniality. Just because one talks

a little. . . okay, a lot. . . should she be deemed an outcast before her peers?

What is that? What's going on? There's a scurry of "klop-klop-klops" in the distance. Do I hear my classmates laughing even behind my back? Something is happening. Is it safe to sneak a peek? How much more trouble can I get into anyway?. . . A note to my parents is a definite, and TALKS TOO MUCH has been marked on my report card three times already.

A peep over my shoulder tells me the coast is clear. Mrs. "V" is nowhere in sight. . . so what is the problem? Why are my classmates covering their mouths and losing themselves in laughter?

I see. As I stare from my corner, a yellow puddle trickles its way out from beneath Kenny B's row #1 desk and winds its way through unlevel floor boards to the front of the room. I overhear Mrs. "V" out in the hallway calling to the janitor that she needs a mop—fast! Poor Kenny B. Suddenly my corner becomes more bearable and secure.

Tammy

Strange whimpering sounds came from the direction of the restaurant kitchen. I had been sitting in the back corner booth, totally occupied with my crayons and coloring book at my mom and dad's small town business when the curious noises began. Even though I was scared, I got up to find the cause, but nothing in the kitchen looked unusual. I thought of one of my mother's sayings. "Your eyes and ears must be playing tricks on you, Judy," and I returned to coloring at my booth again.

Then the whimpers developed more clearly into "mews." Unable to contain my 7-year-old curiosity, I ran behind the counter to find my mother. She stopped her work as I tugged at her apron strings, pleading that she follow me into the kitchen for a search. She reluctantly complied.

There in the small kitchen, Mom and I examined every nook and cranny, even opening the cupboard doors and drawers to find the source of the sounds. Then a barely audible "mew" met my ears again. Tracing its direction, I dropped to the floor and, with my head on the hard, square tiles, scrounged for clues beneath the lowest shelf of the steam table. By now, I guessed that an animal lay hidden some-where nearby. And at last, I spotted it!

Curled into a ball under that steam table, a gaunt but furry kitten clung to her hiding place, far back by the wall. How she got in there, or even into the restaurant in the first place, was hard to understand. The kitten wore sad, frightened eyes. I thought she might try to nip me when I stretched out my arm to reach for her, but she didn't. She appeared weak and helpless, unable to defend herself. As I lay on my side on the floor, I managed to pull her out. Then I sat cross-legged and held her in my hands and arms.

The kitten's whiskers had been cut; she was so thin that I could count her ribs. My heart hurt for the little animal, and I knew I just had to take her home and love her. When I asked Mom and Dad, I thought they might say "no," but they didn't. It looked like they felt sorry for her, too.

In the days ahead, my father even spoiled "Tammy"—with the finest feline food on the grocery shelves. He occasionally bought sardines for her, too, and fattened her up well! As she grew, she developed a beautiful, sleek coat. She lengthened and walked proudly like a princess. Her former shyness had transformed into confidence. Even our fox terrier respected her and hesitated to enter her space uninvited! But she always welcomed tender strokes from Mom, Dad, and me as she purred and snuggled by our ankles.

In spite of the worst circumstances, there is always hope when people care. I learned that at a young age because a scrawny little kitten once entered my life when I was a child.

FRECKLE CREAM!

"Freckles are beautiful!" my mother tried to convince me time and again. Her efforts couldn't match the teasing that I faced from peers, though, and even embarrassing comments from adults. (My uncle used to sing the 1940's song "She's Got Freckles on Her But[t] She's Nice" every time he saw me.)

"You're just saying they're beautiful to make me feel better, Mom. Why can't I get a tan instead of freckles, like everyone else?" Mom just shook her head in exasperation.

Speaking of tanning, I sure did try. But no matter what I did, nothing worked. When I used tanning lotions, I'd only get sunburned, and then my freckles looked even worse. They appeared green in contrast! After one attempt with tanning lotion when I was in middle school, a neighborhood bully passed by on his bike, laughed, and pointed at me as he yelled out to his friends, "Look at the chameleon!" Boy did that hurt.

There were many times I thought, *Why don't my freckles just all join together? Then I won't even have to go out in the sun. I'd have a tan better than everyone else!* But of course, that never happened.

As I entered high school and was even more concerned about my appearance, I knew that somehow, some way, I just had to get rid of my freckles! The solution jumped out at me where I least expected it—at our town's pharmacy and soda fountain. One day, what did I spy on a top shelf of Mr. Ted Sowars's store? A jar labeled "Freckle Cream!"

"What does Freckle Cream do exactly, Mr. Sowars?" I asked.

"It fades out freckles," he replied over his shoulder as he rearranged some items on a nearby shelf.

"Perfect!" I said as I pictured myself with a blemish-free complexion. Granted, I might have to do without a tan, but at least I wouldn't have freckles to worry about anymore.

"Are you thinking about buying this for yourself, Judy?"

"Yes, sir!" was my definite reply.

"I think you should get your mother's permission first, to make sure you're not allergic to any of the ingredients," Mr. Sowars advised, sounding like my grandpa, who happened to be a friend of his.

With that, I set out on a mission, walking across the street to where my mom was waitressing tables at our family's restaurant. Yes! She was busy. There would

be no time for her to think this over a long time or for me to face a major interrogation. But just enough time to convince her to let me buy the Freckle Cream.

"Mom, did you know that there's a special cream Mr. Sowars carries at his store that makes freckles a little lighter, so they don't stand out so much? And it doesn't cost a lot. If you give me a note, Mr. Sowars says I can buy it. Please, Mom? It's just like a nice face cream."

"What does it cost, Judy?"

"Oh, I forget exactly, but I remember it wasn't much, maybe a couple dollars for a big jar," I said.

"Will that make you get over this obsession about your freckles? And will you wait till I look over the jar before you use the cream?" she asked.

"Yes!" I said with delight, knowing I was close to securing the "miracle formula" for ending my life's biggest problem.

Oh, I thought later, *did I forget to tell Mom some things Mr. Sowars said? Oh, well. . .*

Mom handed me a blank check made out to "Sowars' Drug Store" and said that Mr. Sowars could fill in the right amount due for the Freckle Cream. "Remember to get a receipt," she said. Then I was on my way out the restaurant door.

"That was fast," said Mr. Sowars. He pulled down the jar of Freckle Cream, took Mom's check, and gave me the receipt. "Be sure to have your mom read the directions and the warning label, Judy, before you use this," he advised.

That night I planned to apply the cream before going to bed so I could walk into school the next day freckle-free! I was so excited! Mom had so many things on her mind that she forgot all about looking at the label, and I "kind of" forgot to remind her. Before crawling into bed, I rubbed the Freckle Cream extra thick all over my face and arms. I lay down and in no time at all fell asleep to pleasant dreams. I would have beautiful, un-speckled skin in the morning!

"R-R-R-R-ing! R-R-R-R-ing! R-R-R-R-ing!" My alarm went off. I could hear Mom making breakfast in the kitchen as I jumped out of bed and ran to my mirror. My face had been totally transformed, all right. The reflection that greeted me was

that of a red-faced teen with large, ugly welts covering her forehead, her cheeks, and her chin!

"No! This can't be happening!" I screamed, loud enough that Mom heard me two rooms away and came running into the bedroom. She realized immediately what I had done.

I begged to be able to stay home from school that day, but my mother "begged to differ."

"Sorry, honey, you can't skip school. Sometimes we just have to deal with the consequences of our actions," she said.

It was a rough couple days before the redness and welts went away. Some of my classmates must have thought I had the measles or something contagious because they kept their distance.

I never thought I'd say this in a million years, but seeing my freckles finally reappear was a beautiful thing.

A Babysitter's Nightmare

The "Wilsons" were a wonderful family—at least when the kids' mom and dad were around. When I heard the incredible amount they paid their babysitters, I thought, *I can do this*!

The first time I babysat for the family of 8 children, everything went well. We were just getting to know each other. It was about bedtime, so after the older kids finished their homework, and after I worked on reading exercises with the child who was dyslexic, they all settled in for a peaceful night.

The second time I babysat for the Wilsons, true colors began to emerge. While the younger children played in one room, the older children begged to help me make hamburger sandwiches for supper. I wouldn't take any chances on stove burns, but I finally gave in to their pleas to patty the hamburger. What a mistake! They pretended they were making pizzas! They twirled the pattied, raw hamburgers and threw them high into the air. This was an old farmhouse with high ceilings, but the raw hamburgers went all the way up, and parts of them stuck! One of the boys climbed onto the countertop, and using a yardstick, tried to scrape them down—with limited success. Needless to say, we ate smaller sandwiches than originally planned for supper. When the parents came home, I thought they would be upset, but they were unmoved by my report.

A month later I babysat for the Wilsons the third time. The afternoon was uneventful. That night, however, I felt something was going on. I was being purposely sidetracked. While I attended to the younger kids in the living room, I lost sight of 3 of the older boys. Then I smelled it. Smoke!

"Fire! Fire!" The screams came from up the long stairway. I ran up fast to find out what was going on and to get all the kids out of danger. The boys were sitting on the bed in their room, and the mattress had a hole in the middle where it was smoldering! The culprits had lit a lantern on the bed! Should I call the fire department? There were no flames, but there were small sparks. I ordered the kids to get buckets, fill them halfway with water, and we formed a line up the staircase. In a matter of minutes, the situation was resolved. . . other than ruined bed sheets, a smoking mattress, and a sopping wet floor. The boys and I dragged that

mattress down the steps and into the back yard where we packed it with snow. I put the "arsonists" in charge of cleanup, and then they served time standing in living room corners while I collected my senses.

My heart beat fast for the next several hours. There were no cell phones in the 1960's, and I hadn't been left with a landline number. Then the moment I both awaited and dreaded arrived. I heard the parents pull into the driveway. The kids had long been sleeping, some on couches. Mr. and Mrs. Wilson walked in the door.

"I—I—I'm so sorry," I began.

"What's the matter?" asked Mr. Wilson.

"There was a fire. The boys lit a lantern on their bed, and. . . "

"Is everyone okay? "

"Yes, and we dragged the mattress outside and packed the hole with snow, and. . ."

Mr. and Mrs. Wilson looked at each other and smiled! Huh? Shouldn't they be upset? How could they be smiling?

"Oh, honey, don't worry. This isn't the first time the boys have pulled this trick," Mrs. Wilson said. With that, she asked me if I could babysit again the following weekend.

?????? "Uh, I'll have to check my schedule and get back with you," I replied sheepishly.

That was the last time I worked for the Wilsons. A few years later they moved from the area. They might have run out of babysitters.

IF I COULD ONLY REVISIT THAT TIME

We would be sitting in our living room after supper in the early 1960's. Dad would be reading the Sunday issue of the *Dayton Daily News* or a nonfiction book, probably about World War II. Mom, though, would still be scurrying here and there, from the kitchen to the dining room; from the kitchen to the pantry, or from the bedrooms to the laundry pile in the basement until Dad would finally admonish her by nickname to, "Just sit down, Wootz, and take it easy." Then Mom would settle in a living room chair by my dad, in his recliner, and skim the Parade insert section of the newspaper with its entertaining stories and its coupons, which interested her more than the news.

Together, we would watch some TV and talk about the day's events until one of my parents—usually my dad—would nod off into a short early evening nap in the overstuffed chair, feet propped up on the footstool, with eye glasses dangling down his nose. I would be sitting at the dining room table by that time, finishing up the last of my homework for Monday's classes, or I might be lying on the floor in front of the TV, dipping a folded slice of apple butter bread or buttered toast into a cup of hot cocoa.

We might be watching *The Ed Sullivan Show* or *60 Minutes*. Of course, on another night of the week we might be sitting in front of the TV screen watching *The Beverly Hillbillies* and laughing out loud together. If it was after a hot summer day, we would likely be on the back porch steps taking turns cranking the handle on the ice cream maker for some delicious and refreshing homemade ice cream to share with the neighbors. The three of us might be shelling garden peas or snipping beans while watching our programs if we didn't have a chance to finish the garden work in the afternoon.

Yes, I can see it all happening again, and I remember the smells, too. . . the "fresh green" scent of the shelled peas and the snipped beans, the trace of fried sausage, onion, and potatoes lingering in the air from supper, and perhaps the underlying smell of dried sweat after a hot, humid day with no air conditioning. All combined, these things distinguished our home as simply that, our home.

If I could go back in time and see my parents once more, I would ask Mom and Dad a lot of questions, to learn more about their pasts, their feelings, their opinions, and our

family history, knowing with hindsight that our moments together would be precious and fleeting. One of the first questions I'd ask is, "How in the world did Mom ever get the nickname Wootz?" I'd want to say one final "I love you," before my revisiting moments expired. Both of my parents would be gone by the time I reached 26.

When Mom and Dad died, there was grief; now there is nostalgia. I regret that I cannot share memories of my parents with siblings, because I have none, and it hurts that my children never got to know their grandparents while they were alive. But I have the hope that someday my children and grandchildren will feel like they've met Paul and Helen Kaiser through the stories I've told about them and, perhaps, through the longevity of these written words

Small Town...
Gifts of Nature

A Single Firefly

A single firefly escalated,

Lit atop a tree;

While others played their flashlight tag,

He sojourned introspectively,

Searching from that highest twig

To quench his wisdom thirst

As moonbeams danced and shimmered

On the silver-carpeted earth.

Below him nature's opulence;

Above, the universe;

Indelible impressions

Transcending power of words.

Elements so synchronized,

Minutest parts well planned—

And he saw how he, himself, fit in;

A tiny light, but no less grand.

BUTTERFLY

Two colorful leaves

Move with precision.

Antennae protrude

To betray the ploy;

Then the wings

open

and shut midway;

open

and shut midway.

As it inches forward,

It can fool me no more!

A monarch emerges

To rise and to soar.

STUBBY-TAILED SQUIRREL

Comfortably seated in my writing chair,
I glance out the window and pause to stare
At the stubby-tailed squirrel that I consider my friend
Passing through our yard again.

Other squirrels, more endowed than he,
With tails that fly them effortlessly
From branch to branch so gracefully,
Lack my friend's personality.

This little trouper, far from frail,
Though he lacks the others' feathered tails,
Looks the part of a sporadic sprinter
As he rushes to gather his food for winter.

But as our small tomatoes are spotted and picked,
The paths of the squirrel and a cat conflict.
I root for my friend, who finds a hole in a tree,
And I applaud his escape excitedly!

After the mean, prowling feline has fled,
It's back to the garden for a rotten cabbage head.
The brown furry squirrel fills his cheeks in a hurry,
Nipping and gnawing, then away he scurries.

His next mission's set—fruit from our tree,

And off he goes, with an apple in his teeth.

The sight is amusing, but craziest of all

Is when my frisky little friend finds a missing tennis ball!

Unshaken by its size, he's resolved as he can be.

That quirky, jerky squirrel is on a "Finders Keepers" spree!

He drags it through the yard, determined in his labors;

He takes that ball across the alley, over to the neighbors'!

He hauls it up their maple tree to stash his newfound treasure;

As I follow his persistence, I'm impressed beyond all measure.

My determined little buddy has met his challenge of the day,

But I doubt he's let anything ever stand in his way—

Not a tail that's stubby or a cat that's mean,

Tennis balls, apples, or cabbage head leaves;

What an unstoppable squirrel, an extraordinary critter,

Who goes after his goals—an achiever, not a quitter!

THE RAIN INSIDE

Thunder rumbles;
Light subsides.
Impending raindrops
No longer hide.
They dot the glass panels;
They break loose from the pane
To stream down profusely
As clouds unleash the rain.

There's a Sparrow Out Back

There's a sparrow out back

With no place to go.

Bird homes are filled to capacity.

While wrens and martins are singing away,

He's unnoticed, shown no hospitality.

He's simple; he's common,

A bit charming and sweet,

And though talent appears to be lacking,

He's refreshingly humble in a world full of pride,

With its fine-feathered flaunting and bragging.

DANDELIONS

(*Begun in collaboration with my 6th graders, 1999)

White puffs of cotton

Shoot from cushiony hubs

That balance on green-tubed stems

As young lips

Blow wisps of air

To send the delicate stars

Rising

Floating

Into the summer sky

Acrobat Squirrel

Acrobat squirrel, hanging upside down,

You suspend yourself crazily close to the ground,

Entertaining yourself with your bagful of tricks,

Chat-ter-ing sassiness and clickety clicks.

Dangling an acorn between tiny claws,

You gnaw away, play away—then instantly PAUSE.

An intruder's been sighted. He's spoiling your fun!

From my window it looks like your antics are done.

But you scale up the tree to precarious height,

Leaping wiry limbs from site to site.

When your chaser gives up in exasperation,

You chit-ter delight at the cat's frustration;

Then twitter your tail to mock the feline below—

And with that grand finale, you close your show!

Summer Rain

$\mathcal{W}$et, hot pavement cools
Where rainbow colors hover.
Leaves sparkle with crystal beads;
Grass dons a diamond cover.

Life's refreshed by summer rain;
A glimpse of heaven comes to Earth.
A revived sun pours out its gold,
And Nature glistens in its rebirth.

ANT HILL

A

brown

sandy mound;

here the workers toil

up and down the crevices

in hardened, sun-baked soil,

hauling burdens twice their size

with unyielding determination

as they go about their labor

focused on their mission;

working all together,

they finish the task,

retreating to rest

at last.

MAYDROPS

S carlet hearts tightly woven in bud,

Balance aloft a single stem

And summon thirsty leaves,

Palms upraised,

To catch the sparkling sustenance.

Small Town...
Family Life

What's in a Name?

My aunt, Marie Kaiser, married Charlie Keaser. She became Marie Kaiser Keaser. Another aunt, originally Jeannie Keiser, married Uncle Jack and became Jeannie Keiser Kaiser. I'm happy I didn't end up marrying a nice young man in my hometown whose last name was "Jutte," or I would be called Judy Jutte.

I married, instead, a "Paul," but my dad's name was "Paul," and I felt funny calling my hubby by my dad's name so I've often called him by his nickname, "Wac." That makes sense, doesn't it?

The problem is, my husband has two younger brothers who have also been called "Wac," so there's "Big Wac," "Middle Wac," and "Little Wac." But actually, "Little Wac" has become known by most people as "Ace," so that helps prevent confusion, doesn't it? Anyway, now I'm hoping my Wac (Big Wac), a gifted cook, will someday open a Chinese restaurant. I already know what we'll call it—"Wac's Wok"—what a perfectly fitting name.

WHAT'S IN THE GLASS?

My husband and I were on a date night at the Eagles Club in our town when Paul introduced me to Clarence, who invited us to sit down and join him for a bite to eat and a drink. Two things about him immediately caught my attention—his subtle sense of humor and that he seemed slightly cross-eyed.

Clarence initiated the conversation. He certainly was congenial enough. Everyone appeared to know him and smiled as they passed by. Then something happened that would be difficult for me to forget.

I caught sight of an object in Clarence's glass. Shock! Floating in his drink was an eyeball! A human eyeball! My heart did a triple flip! I gasped, but when I tried to speak, my words got caught in my throat.

Clarence, my husband, and everyone else around us broke into laughter. After my husband settled down, he pointed to the object in his friend's drink and said, "It's his glass eye. He does this all the time."

With a smile, Clarence picked up his scotch and water and finished it. Then he lifted the glass eyeball from the bottom, wiped it off, and without a flinch, inserted the eyeball back into its socket.

As I sought to regain my composure, the conversation resumed, but not without suspicion. Would Clarence strike again? Who would become the next unwary victim of this prankster's joke?

A Prestigious Golf Award

Playing golf was not my favorite activity, but it was an excuse for a "date night" with my husband, so I accompanied him a few times to a local course owned by friends. On one occasion I applauded the fact that, at least in my opinion, I had done a fairly decent job that day—meaning I usually hit the ball on the first swing and that it usually landed on the course somewhere between the hole and me. My hubby's and my golfing date came to an abrupt end, however, when the clouds overhead did not pass by as expected but unleashed a sudden downpour of rain. Paul and I jumped in the golf cart and headed for shelter.

When we exited the cart by the clubhouse, clumsy me—wearing white pants and a t-shirt—lost my balance and fell into a mud puddle. Much to my embarrassment, I saw that I had an audience watching from the clubhouse windows.

Imagine my husband's and my surprised delight when several weeks later we received an invitation to attend the annual golf club's banquet free of charge! Paul and I both thought that he had a chance to be honored as "Most Improved" since he felt his game had gradually gotten better.

The evening of the golf awards banquet arrived. My husband and I were led to our reserved seats. Following a delicious 3-course meal, names were announced for awards. I exchanged a questioning look with the man sitting to one side of me when we were both called to the stage!

"Do you know what this is about?" I asked.

"I have no idea," he replied. "Are you a good golfer?"

My husband didn't wait for me to reply. He shook his head to a definite, "No!"

As my table friend and I stood on stage in suspense, the fun-loving host of the golf awards banquet tried in vain to suppress a smile. He complimented the two of us for our diligence, but then in the next breath he challenged us to try our hand at a different sport. Everyone broke out in laughter as my friend and I opened our gift-wrapped packages. We had each been awarded a – KITE!

FINDING TIME

Beds were made in the morning;

Children were dressed for the day.

Meal's been prepared for our family;

Cleaned dishes are stacked away.

Laundry's been washed and folded;

The house must be cleaned yet this week.

Mending and ironing amount to a pile full;

Baked cookies are ready to eat!

Jonny comes in 'cuz he's thirsty;

The dog's tracked mud in the den!

The neighbor kids' play is rehearsed, underway;

This one-woman audience attends.

Thank you, dear Lord, for needs I may fill

And for the moments still found in this tizzy

To listen, to watch, to play with the kids

When it's so tempting to say, "I'm too busy."

What's That, Cat?

What's that, cat?—You've gone too far!
A farmer's lot for you!
First hissin', then plompin', then serenadin' past two;
Your Romeo days are just about through!

Been bustin' my britches for this family of mine;
A body needs sleep when thar's meals on the line,
So take your romancin' an' dancin' instead
'Neath another one's window while I'm still in bed!

THE HAIRCUT

Our daughter Carmen had the most beautiful long hair. It flowed halfway down her back in waves of gold. "What lovely hair your daughter has!" everyone would say to my husband and me, and they were right. It really was.

In kindergarten, Carmen wore her hair high in pigtails. They framed her happy face, and each one touched her shoulders in a curl.

In first grade, she had a ponytail. I would tie a ribbon around the top of it and let the ends of the ribbon trail down the sides of Carmen's neck. She looked so cute!

Sometimes I put Carmen's hair up, on the very top of her head. Once when her dance class performed on a stage, a crown of flowers adorned her hairdo, too.

In second grade, Carmen wore sparkly headbands. She let her long, wavy hair fall sweetly behind her ears, with all but a few swirls down the side of her cheeks.

Then, when she turned eight, it was time for a trim. My husband and I were not well off financially, so I decided to cut Carmen's hair just a little bit, myself. "I want you to sit straight and tall on the kitchen chair," I said. "Be careful to hold very still so the scissors don't slip."

First, I snipped the right side, then the left side, but the golden hair was not cut straight across, so I tried again.

I snipped a tiny bit from the right side this time, and a bit more from the left. Her hair still was not cut straight across.

Then I cut a little bit more. . . a little bit more. . . then some more. . . till, finally, the job was done. I stood back to look at Carmen's haircut. Much to my surprise, my daughter's hair was now cropped shorter than I had intended. . . much, much shorter! The golden waves and curls lay on the kitchen floor.

Oh, no! What have I done! I thought.

Sensing something was wrong, Carmen put her hands to her head and let her fingers comb through the locks she thought were there. She turned in her chair and stared at the floor, then rushed to the bathroom to look in the mirror. I stood in the

kitchen still holding the scissors when she returned to ask with confusion, "Mom, why did you cut off so much? I thought you were just going to trim it."

I faked a smile and told her how nice she looked in short hair, but my heart sank as I swept up my daughter's waves and curls from the floor. With that finished, I sneaked to the bedroom and sobbed.

When my husband came home from work, he could read the emotion on my face. He looked across the room to see our daughter and the missing long hair. It wasn't hard to figure what had happened. His two girls were feeling pretty low. His attempt to make us feel better didn't help much. "It will grow back," he said, but the time I knew it would take, seemed an eternity.

*   *   *

Fast forward many years. Carmen's beautiful hair did grow back, though never quite as long and flowing as before. The "extreme" childhood haircut, however, did not impact her growth in other respects. It did not stop our daughter from getting good grades and showing athletic ability in high school. It did not stop her from going on to college and, after graduation, marrying a wonderful man and having three boys and a girl— all but one of college age now. Our granddaughter, like her mother, does very well in college and has outstanding athletic ability. Today, as Carmen's daughter dashes around the track at NCAA competitions, her long, golden hair streams behind her in waves as she flies to the finish line.

I've learned with age that time carries with it some ironies and has its own way of smiling at past mistakes. I see my granddaughter. . . and I feel the weight of my guilty burden subside. It's almost as if our daughter's beautiful, flowing locks have been restored.

Wisecracks in the Kitchen

Our son Jon is a very fine cook who also surprises us occasionally with his subtle sense of humor. He comes up with a line "out of nowhere" and turns a mundane situation into a side-splitting, brainy joke.

One day he stood in the kitchen conscientiously slicing a roasted chicken by the stove, under a bright, overhead light. He was obviously being careful to cut and separate all the pieces precisely. I was working in the kitchen at the same time and asked him a question. He kept his eyes on what he was doing and didn't respond.

I thought he hadn't heard me so I asked the question again. He looked up from the knife and the chicken, and with an ornery grin said, "Sh-sh-sh! I'm performing a breast reduction."

Good Intentions

Our eight-year-old son Dan had good cleaning intentions, but things didn't always turn out right. One day when I checked out a strong smell that was spreading throughout the house, I walked into the bathroom to find Dan scrubbing the family dog in the tub. I leaned over our son's shoulder to see what kind of shampoo he was using. At that moment, the pooch lost all composure. He squirmed out of Dan's grip, shaking a spray of water over everything. Then, sneezing uncontrollably, the dog slid across the linoleum floor and out the door to his freedom.

Before chasing him down with a towel, I fixed my eyes on the source of the dog's desperation. There, on the edge of the tub, sat the bottle of pungent "shampoo" my son had been using. It wasn't shampoo at all! It was a powerful, disinfectant household cleaner labelled "Lysol!"

Dan patted me on the back and tried to console my frustration. "It's okay, Mom. Look at it this way—I'll bet I got rid of Barney's fleas!"

Yes, I'll bet you did, I thought, *but the poor dog might not come out of hiding for some time to come.*

* * * *

Another "good intentions" bathroom incident occurred when Dan wanted to surprise me with his house cleaning efforts. He remained quiet about his work until everything was completed. Then he invited me into the bathroom for an inspection of the finished product.

"Look at the sink, Mom. See how clean it is?" It appeared he had done a fine job.

"Look at the toilet, Mom. See how shiny it is?" The toilet seat, indeed, glistened as never before.

"How did you get everything to sparkle so, Dear?" I asked out of genuine curiosity.

"Well," he answered, "We were out of the stuff you use, so I just used this," he said, holding up a bottle of floor wax! The only place he hadn't used it was on the bathroom floor. I stood there hoping no one would slide off the toilet seat before I had a chance to "re-do" Dan's work.

HER FIRST CAR
THE "ORANGE BOMBER"

"I got a real bargain for you, Carmen! Let's take it out for a test drive!" my husband said as he pointed to the bright orange "tank" of an automobile he had just pulled into the driveway. It was to be a surprise gift for our daughter, her very first 2nd-hand car, to celebrate passing her driver's test.

I stood on the sidewalk, traumatized. *Oh, my. This "monstrosity" will be in our driveway for years to come.* It was not a pleasant thought.

"It's built strong, has low mileage, and should last you a long time," Paul said. He pointed to the vehicle with pride. "It's sleek, too."

Hm-m-m. . . Sleek? I looked at its body and, yes, I had to agree that the car had smooth lines along the sides, at least from the front door to the rear, but everything else was massive. Its bulging front fenders resembled a prop plane, with huge headlights on the propeller engines. The tail lights protruded from the back like a busty woman in reverse. I looked over at our daughter for her reaction.

It took a while for the shock to subside. "For Me? You sure, Dad? I could just borrow our family car once in a while . . .Really. . ."

"Nope. This one's all for you. Hop in. I'll show you how to work the controls."

Carmen obediently seated herself in the passenger side of her "new" orange automobile. Her father started driving it around the block, turning the windshield wipers on and off; testing the headlights; trying out the horn. I lost sight of our daughter's expressions through her car window. It looked like she was trying to shield her face as they passed down the street of our neighborhood.

That was the beginning of the "orange bomber" saga in our family, but thankfully the car didn't last as long as feared. Carmen saved her money to buy a more "respectable" vehicle a couple years later for college. Her father, for the life of him, couldn't understand why. The orange bomber, subsequently, got passed down to our son Jon for a short while, but he said the seats were uncomfortable and the car lost power, so it was sold.

Our youngest son, Dan, totally escaped the inheritance.

Grandma's Park

When the grandkids came over to visit years ago, they liked to go to the town's park, only half a block from our house. Jackie, Mark, Maa-Maa (Matt), and Jay-Jay (Jason), called it "Grandma's Park."

We walked and we skipped to the playground area, passing a lot of activity along the way. Parents rooted for their 10-year-olds on the park's baseball diamond. Teens played basketball on the asphalt court, and while little kids scuffled a soccer ball across grass still sparkling with morning dew, Jackie, Mark, Maa-Maa, Jay-Jay, and I began having our own fun. We glided into the air on the swings. We squealed down the slides. We pushed up and down on the teeter-totters, sometimes trying to bounce our partner off their seat, and we squished our wriggling, bare toes in the wide box of sand and made pictures in it with a stick. Then it was time to go home.

That was "Grandma's Park"—The name had a sort of precious sound to it years ago, at least to me, and I'm sure it always will.

WATCHING JACKIE RUN!

We're nervous

 Restless

Excitedly senseless

All eyes are set on her

As she rounds the corner

She leaps the last hurdle

We hoot and we holler

She's FIRST at the FINISH!

With joy undiminished

We're hugging and screaming

The track coach is beaming

There's nothing more fun

Than watching Jackie run!

GRANDMA'S RECLINING READING CHAIR
*FOR EVA

Grandma Judy reads to me

In her big reclining chair,

Her walker propped beside it

While stories take us everywhere.

We surf the waves in oceans;

Drive camels through desert sands;

Take rickshaws past Chinese pagodas;

Steer sleds over ice-covered lands.

We climb up the Eiffel Tower,

We ski down a mountain peak.

We ride the range on broncos;

Then we drift into Dreamland,

My sleepy head

On Grandma's cheek.

Our Dog Barney and the Pesky Fly

With cunning poise, Barney eyeballed his target—silently, patiently—as a blood-thirsty native prepares to thrust his spear. Every muscle and limb attended to a motionless stance. Only his eyes moved as they followed the naïve, buzzing nuisance circling overhead.

That which was airborne prepared to land on the polished edge of a round, mahogany table below. "Dangerous territory," I muttered from my reading chair, newspaper lowered to my lap. The fly came to a rest only twelve paw-lengths from Barney's muzzle. Placing odds on my canine's speed and skill, I became transfixed on the silent spectacle, which time had staged just for me.

Then, calm and collected, the hound seized his chance! In a split second's flash, a well executed lunge found him snatching the fly, completely off guard, from the site. Leap!—Open!—Chomp!—Gone!

Nature's sport ended as nonchalantly as it had begun, 'cept for one thing. Barney left the room a bit more satisfied having had the experience.

DECK OF CARDS

Circle of six,

Just sitting around;

Nothing's going on

Till the cards are found.

They're shuffled and dealt;

The silence ends

With aces and deuces

As the game begins!

There's talking and laughing,

Recalling good times.

When the clock chimes the hour,

We pay it no mind.

For family and friends,

All problems depart

When someone brings out

A deck of cards!

GOODBYE, GOOD FRIEND

Our shiny, black Labrador hadn't eaten for several days. Now she wasn't drinking from her water bowl either. Something was wrong. We couldn't blame it on a case of stomach flu anymore. My husband decided it was time to take her to the vet.

I'll never forget that day. Paul put the leash on the dog and walked her two blocks to Dr. Slavik's office. There my husband would be told the cause of Maggie's illness, the dog would be given some medicine or a shot, and Paul would bring her back home for some rest. It would be that simple, or so we thought.

Time went by. Finally, I saw my husband rounding the corner at the end of the block. I walked out on the porch to greet him. He was carrying Maggie's collar and leash, but our dog was not with him. *Dr. Slavik is keeping her overnight for observation,* I thought, surprised at the possibility she was sicker than we had expected. I inquired of Paul to make sure.

"Where's the dog?" I asked. He didn't look up at me. He just kept on walking toward the house, head bowed. "Where's Maggie?" I asked again, assuming he had not heard me the first time.

"Just leave me alone. I need to be alone." With that, he dashed into the backyard, tears flowing down his cheeks, and I followed. I couldn't leave him alone. Yes, Maggie was my husband's hunting partner, but she belonged to us all. She was part of our family—a companion to our children, a playmate to their neighborhood friends.

"Paul, pull yourself together," I said. "Tell me what happened. Where's our dog?"

"She's gone," he said simply.

"What do you mean 'she's gone'?" I was getting frustrated with my husband's half answers. "Is the doctor keeping Maggie for observation?"

"She's dead. She had cancer in her throat really bad. There was too much pain. Slavik thought it best to put her to sleep." At that point my husband lost his composure and begged again, "Just let me be alone awhile." And I did.

Walking back to the house, I sat down at the kitchen table and buried my head in my arms, trying to come to grips with the shock. Before I could regain my own composure, five-year-old Dan walked into the kitchen. He saw me distraught, struggling to keep it together. Puzzled, he looked up at me and asked, "What's wrong, Mommy? You sad about something?"

Still finding it hard to speak intelligibly, I mustered the words to explain. "Dan," I said, "Maggie was very sick. The animal doctor put her to sleep."

Our son listened, staring at me with eyes open wide. Then he turned and casually walked out the patio door to, he said, play with his friends. I thought the news about our dog's death would need some time to settle in.

An hour passed. My husband was still not back from a drive he had taken to reflect on the day. As I stood at the kitchen sink, lethargically, pensively, struggling to do dishes while I stared out the window, Dan came running in the back door.

"Why did you lie to me, Mom?! Maggie's not sleeping. She's dead!" He was bawling uncontrollably, and in his frenzy, he clenched his fingers and swung his hands in the air.

Now it became clear. How could I have made such a mistake? Dan had thought our dog, his life-long buddy, as old as he, was sleeping overnight at the "dog hospital." When he told one of the neighbor kids Maggie was being put to sleep, the boy replied, "He's not really asleep, Silly. That means your dog is dead."

I reached out to my boy's hands and clutched them in my own hands. "It'll be okay, Dan. It hurts bad, but it'll be okay."

We sat on the kitchen floor, my son and I, hugging each other, crying. Our family had lost a very good friend. We'd need to get through this together.

Yuck! That Candy Didn't Taste Good!

As relatives, friends, and I left the baby shower, we gave our good-bye hugs, and I drove home. After pulling in the driveway and walking into the house, the Thank You favor from the hosts, a small box containing two luscious butterfly cookies and a cellophane pouch with a candy star in it, seemed too yummy to resist any longer. *How creative*, I thought. *The candy star is pale lavender, the same shade Andrea said the baby's bedroom walls will be painted. Candy sounds so good right now*, I thought, and I plopped the piece in my mouth.

"Oh! Oh! Yuck!! Oh-h-h!!" I ran to the kitchen wastebasket and spit it out! Then I Spit! Spit! some more, but no matter how many times I tried to get rid of the horrible taste, I couldn't get it out of my mouth soon enough. In panic, I rinsed with glass after glass of water. It took forever, it seemed, until the disgusting aftertaste lessened and became tolerable.

Finally, I sniffed the cellophane wrapper and examined the lavender chunk in the wastebasket. Reality sank in. I had taken a bite out of a "star" of perfumed sachet! As I discovered later—too late—a warning had been given by the hosts at the baby shower to NOT eat the lavender star in the quaint little cellophane wrapper because it was meant to be hung in a closet! I had been having so much fun talking with the ladies at my table that I hadn't heard the instructions.

I phoned my daughter and sister-in-law to warn them, only to find that they had not even picked up the Thank You favors as they left the shower, as I had. Needless to say, there were some jokes directed my way in the weeks that followed, and the embarrassing incident was added to my storehouse of gaffes.

YOU BRING ME PATIENCE

*DEDICATED TO DONNIE, WHOSE SPECIAL NEEDS
PROVIDE FOR MY SPECIAL NEEDS

You bring me patience.

All those blessings

I've often walked by,

Taking no heed,

You help me now to see.

And in the rush

Of my daily life,

You silently say to

"Slow down"...

To take some time

To care, to love,

And to thank my Lord

For people like you

Who prune other people

like me.

Small Town...
Teacher Tales

Mrs. Tinkler

"Mrs. Tinkler" required respect from her students and other teachers alike. Then one day my co-workers and I saw it— a long stream of toilet paper trailing from under her skirt as she walked from the school bathroom and approached her classroom down the hall. The other teachers and I stood dumbfounded in the hallway, wondering who would spot the problem first— Mrs. Tinkler OR the students awaiting her return.

Luckily for Mrs. Tinkler, the toilet paper disengaged as it caught on her classroom doorstop. My feelings of inferiority in her presence, however, changed after that day. Every time I saw Mrs. Tinkler, I remembered the trail of toilet paper dragging behind her. I now understood that she was vulnerable to embarrassment like everyone else.

Follow The Bouncing Eyeball

One day between classes, I found an unusual item on the classroom floor. It was a hollow, aluminum novelty toy that looked just like a bloodshot eyeball. I came up with an idea—I'd pull a joke on the other 6th grade teachers who were chatting out in the hall while our students were having recess.

I fit the aluminum eyeball into the space between my right eyebrow and my cheekbone, next to my nose. Then I squinted to hold the fake eyeball in place. I walked out into the hall with my hand over my right eye, complaining of an excruciating headache. Then, according to plan, I withdrew my cupped hand from my face, and the fake eyeball dropped from my socket! "Oh no! My eye! My eye!" I shrieked in alarm. My colleagues pulled back in shock as the fake eyeball bounced down the hallway! . . . But the story doesn't end there.

I laughed so hard that my blood pressure shot up, and I became dizzy. The other teachers put me in my desk chair and wheeled me down the hall to the elevator, then down to the first floor where they rolled me into the nurse's station. From there, I was taken to the hospital emergency room, where I recovered later that day. The most embarrassing moments of the whole ordeal came when I had to explain to the E.R. doctor what put me in the emergency room in the first place. . . and then facing the other 6th grade teachers with their "eye" jokes upon my return.

I kept the "eyeball" in my classroom desk drawer till I retired, as a reminder to think twice before pulling another practical joke—at least one that might backfire.

MY CONTRIBUTION TO SCIENCE

Our cooks' culinary skills were magnificent. Rather than pack my lunch, I regularly ate cafeteria food. Being a slow eater, I would take my tray to my classroom so I could eat leisurely and grade papers at the same time.

It was the last day of school before Christmas break when I was pokier than usual; I hadn't finished my delicious holiday meal by the time students entered the classroom from recess. I was determined to eat the chicken legs, the corn, and my roll later, in-between classes, so I shoved my tray into the tall cabinet next to my desk and shut the cabinet door.

Two and a half weeks later, the day before students would return from Christmas break, the custodian greeted me as I came to prepare my classroom. "I have a little surprise for you," he said, and I wondered what it could be. He walked over to my desk, opened the cabinet door next to it, and pulled out the long-forgotten tray. *Moldy* is an understatement. My food was growing hair!

With a smirky glow, Bob remarked, "I was drawn to your cabinet by a peculiar odor, and then I found this wonderful specimen for Mrs. Thomas. She welcomes contributions for her science experiments."

By the next day, the other teachers were smacking their lips and asking how I enjoyed my Christmas meal. It was one of those blunders I would never live down.

WHAT WE DO WITH WHAT WE'VE GOT

Some students are self-motivated; others aren't and need an extra boost. Some people change with time; others see no need.

Over a span of 35 years, I substitute taught throughout the county and taught full time at two schools. Like other teachers, my experiences included interaction with a variety of student personalities. Most students were cooperative and ready to learn; many an utter joy to teach; a few, however, made teaching a bit of a challenge.

There is one particularly challenging school year I will never forget. As I walked into the classroom on the first day after summer break, a student lay, belly down, squirming around on top of his desk. This was followed by a stomping noise approaching from the hallway stairwell, after which student #2 bolted into the room still bursting with energy. *Oh, my! I hope this is not the norm of what's to come,* I remember thinking. Next, student #3, who had been slouching back low in his chair, began sliding off—till the first period bell startled him to attention, at least temporarily. Certainly not lacking in variety, my new class, I was told ahead of time, featured student #4 who had a tendency to "lift" things—like in "stealing."

Needless to say, keeping this class focused and engaged was challenging that year, not only for me but for all the grade level teachers and, in retrospect, the situation had to be equally exasperating for the students' highly motivated peers. When the last day of school finally came around, however, I felt confident that despite trying times, a great deal of progress had been made overall.

After many years had passed by, I ran across my fellow, former educators who remembered this famed, "diversified" group from the 80's. . . Had my cohorts heard anything about them since the students graduated? Did the kids change at all? I wondered.

"Well, yes and no," said a friend.

I learned that the two extraordinarily-active students turned out to be successful businessmen in their communities. The under-active student eventually got some "get-up-and-go" and fared well, too. All did fine, except our little "thief" who, in spite of help from teachers and others who took him under wing, carried on with his preoccupation, got caught and served some time.

Following that conversation, my fellow retired teachers and I reminisced more about the "old days" and our former students. Many had become respected citizens and contributors in their communities. Hoping that the same outcome would hold true for others who piqued my interest, I inquired about two students who had boasted high IQs but who did little or no work for other teachers or myself. I learned that, today, one of those students holds a steady job in a factory and seems quite content. The other is a cashier and routinely nods off while waiting on customers. All night video games, I was told, were to blame.

For what it's worth, my classroom experiences and practical observations have led me to a simple conclusion. Some of us get motivated to better ourselves over time; others don't. But no matter how we start off, where we end up depends on what we decide to do with what we've got.

BE CAREFUL WHAT YOU REVEAL

One morning I made the mistake of telling my students that yawning is contagious, that I couldn't see someone do it without doing it myself. That afternoon, when I turned around from a writing lesson on the marker board, everyone in class faked a yawn. That precipitated one on my part—then on their part—then on my part, AND SO ON. . .until finally, the classroom erupted into side-holding laughter!

The principal walked by in the hallway and poked his head in the door to see what was going on. I tried to get my composure. "It started with a yawn," I explained, after which he left in utter confusion.

Animal Bribery in the Classroom

Another blot of humor on my professional career developed the day I revealed my "talent"—No, not that I used to play an accordion in a high school "swing band." It was my ability to imitate animal sounds. My students were skeptical at first, but curious. They wanted to hear for themselves. I used their curiosity and my (limited) imitations as a bribe: If everyone in class completed their homework for the next day, I promised to reward them by imitating a sheep.

It worked! Everyone walked into the room the following day with homework completed! In keeping my promise, I bellowed out a long and vibrant, "Ba-a-a-a-!" The class went into hysterics!

On Tuesday the homework bribe was for barking and howling like a dog. It worked again! All assignments were completed on Wednesday, and I stuck to my word, complying with a "Bow-wow-bowwow-ahooh-ahoohh!"

As days passed, my class heard a rooster crowing, a feline meowing (and hissing), and an agitated cow mooing. Before long, in addition to my students, I was acquiring an audience of teachers in the hallway outside my door! In order to return a degree of sanity to my classroom and to focus attention back to education in our middle school building, it was obvious that something had to change.

Eventually I narrowed down my bribing animal calls to only two days per school year—the day before Christmas break and the last day of the school year. It was then, during the very last minute before their departure, that students would come by my classroom for the most highly requested, bleating sheep—which remained the traditional sendoff favorite until I retired.

PLEASE LEAD

My seventh graders welcomed the invitation to lead the reading of short stories. It entitled some lucky student the right to sit in the towering, prestigious director's chair at the front of the room. However, one day when I invited Brandon to lead, he looked at me sheepishly. I gave him the go ahead again, "Please, lead."

I went to the back of the room to erase the board, then turned around to see why the story hadn't started. My reader was nowhere to be seen! I asked the class, "Where's Brandon?"

Replies came simultaneously, "He's in the hall."

Heading toward the classroom door, I asked aloud, "He left the room without permission?"

One of my students responded, "But, Mrs. Bruns, you told him to leave."

Following an unsuccessful attempt to restrain my laughter, joined by the students when they realized the misunderstanding, too, I went out to get the boy. He walked back in with hesitation, but only after I repeatedly assured him that he had done nothing wrong.

THE OBJECT OF ENVY

From 4 years of age to my late 30's, I can honestly say that I loved skating. I could never wait to get moving on that roller rink floor to show off my skills. So for my 37th birthday, my husband, knowing his wife's favorite recreational activity, purchased new precision dancing wheels for my 24-year-old boot roller skates. I couldn't have been happier.

The next day, in the hallway between classes at school, my teacher friends gathered around me wanting to know, "So, WHAT did your husband get you for your birthday?"

I answered them with excitement. "A brand new set of wheels!"

Oh, you should have seen their faces. They looked at me with pure envy. I hadn't realized, they must have liked skating, too.

L.A. Rap

L.A. teachers hold the key

To writing and speaking effectively.

Communication is essential today,

At home, at school, and in the business place.

With fine vocab and skill with grammar,

You can dazzle your peers with your intelligent manner.

You read fine books about adventure and strife

To understand more about this thing called "life."

You can land a job with impressive pay!

Your boss will marvel at the things you say!

Over all the "subjects" language arts is "king."

It equips us all

To better "do our thing!"

Small Town...
Life Lessons Along the Way

ONE FORD TAURUS VS. ONE CROSSING DOE

It had happened to other motorists in our area. I read about it occasionally in the newspaper, but never paid it much mind. I didn't realize how frightening the situation could be.

As my vehicle moved at the speed limit down the highway, two glowing eyes suddenly stared into my headlights. My wheels were aimed at a deer.

There she stood, remarkably calm, in the middle of the road. Direct impact would likely send me to a hospital; if I slowed or swerved my car too abruptly, I risked an accident, too. My options flew before me in a fraction of a second.

As my adrenaline peaked, I applied the brakes assertively, but cautiously, to avoid losing control and rolling my car. My attention went from the deer to the highway ahead, to the shoulder, to the field that stretched off on the right. With no oncoming traffic, I geared my Ford Taurus into the left lane. To my relief, the deer broke her gaze and leaped off the road into the ditch on the right.

The scene plays back in my mind each time I drive my car past a wooded area or cornfields where I now know danger could be lurking. Only a couple inches had separated my car from extensive damage and, possibly, both the deer's life and mine from coming to an end.

NICK'S JOY

It's interesting, the effect that a stuffed animal toy can have on a person—especially on someone who's dependent on others for life's basic needs. I found that to be the case one day in the corridor of our local nursing home.

Nick is an upper-middle-aged, mentally and physically challenged person who often wanders the hallways with his walker. During my visits at the nursing home a few years ago, I never saw Nick smile, and I wondered if he even could. Then an idea "popped" into my mind. I remembered leafing through a catalog and seeing a page of stuffed animal toys that made sounds when they were squeezed. One of the furry toys, quite life-like, was a cat that purred and "meowed." I wondered if a meowing, purring, stuffed cat might be just what was needed to liven Nick up a bit! When asked, the nursing staff agreed that I could give it a try.

It was quite a treat for the nurses, the aides, and me that December day when Nick "met" his cat for the first time. Despite his palsy, Nick managed to hold the cat up, examine it, and go through the motions of deciding what to do with the thing. At first, it looked like he might just pitch it onto the floor, but then, as he held the cat by its tail, something must have "clicked" in his heart. Nick pulled the cat closer and put it in his walker basket. As hoped, after that first meeting he and his cat became inseparable.

Nick learned how to make the stuffed animal purr, and how to make it meow. Once, when the aides forgot to put the cat in Nick's walker basket, I went to his room and got it for him. As soon as he saw his cat, Nick's lips developed into a broad smile, and then he laughed. He reached for his cat, held it to his chest and hugged it with tenderness, kind of like a daddy with his newborn child.

Some time later when I visited friends at the nursing home, Nick and his feline companion were travelling the hallway. Nick's face was glowing with joy. I wondered if it was the stuffed cat that had made the difference. I like to think, though, that something bigger was involved. Roles were reversed in Nick's situation. <u>He</u> had become a caregiver. . . And there's something very special about feeling needed.

PRECIOUS CHILD

Precious child, all beaten up,
Goes upstairs to hide.
His mind and heart can't understand—
"What makes them do this? Why?"

His dad is jobless, can't provide;
Beer only adds to the sting.
His mom works hard; ain't enough, though,
To quench her thirst for expensive things.

"You cry like a baby! Toughen up!"
Their words hurt more than his skin,
But he keeps the secret so they'll be safe;
So police won't lock them in.

Precious Child, oh, blameless child!
Look out your window to see
Sunbeams dancing on puddles of rain
Making rainbows on oil-stained streets!

Tell someone. There's hope and help.
God doesn't want you to live this way,
Where upside-down values come with a cost,
But should an innocent child be the one who pays?

Rising Above the Pain with Humility

*A*wake from sleep,

I rolled to my side,

To sit at the edge of the bed,

Praying I might be provided relief

From pain in the day ahead.

An aching surged

Down my back as I stood;

Then the legs I'd depended upon

Refused to lift me, to hold me, to move me.

Tears began building; independence was gone.

With confidence fleeing;

Now humbled by needs

That I, alone, could not face,

At my lowest, my friends stepped in

To fill all of my needs with their grace.

MEDALS ON THE WALL

Tim points to the dangling "appreciation" medals that span his nursing home wall. A collage of framed photos confirms his claim of being the #1 fan of his hometown high school team over the years. When he wasn't assisting with stats, Tim "Clipboard" James could be found on a bottom bleacher watching the Cavaliers take on their competitors in basketball, in baseball, or at Friday night football games in the stadium. One photo in particular captures my attention. In it, Tim, hunched from childhood polio, stands balanced without his walker, next to the football players and their legendary coach, John Reed.

At the mention of Reed's name, Tim gets teary-eyed. "He was the best. I miss him," he tells me. A high school guidance counselor, a part-time pastor in his church, and a model of character for his football players, Reed took Tim under wing. "About everybody thought the world of him. He was a good man," Tim says, revealing more about himself and his own soft heart at age 60 than he realizes. Then he looks at me and adds, "A part of me went with Coach Reed when he died."

Changing the topic to brighten his mood, I ask, "Would you like to go for a 'spin' and do some visiting?"

"Sure," he answers as he unlocks the lever on each side, and I start pushing him forward in his wheelchair. We roll down the halls to drop in on another ardent sports fan in the nursing home, someone who shares Tim's additional regard for the Cincinnati Reds and the Bengals. Melvin moves his walker out of the way of our entry and welcomes us in. The two sports enthusiasts start talking players and team standings immediately.

After a while, Tim and I head back across the atrium and down the long hallways to his room. We stop at the snack counter along the way, per his request, for a bag of his favorite M & M candies and a can of Pepsi Cola. He assures me that the nurses say his diabetes is under control; that there's no reason for guilt in getting him sweets. So why do I feel like an accomplice when we wheel into his room and he whispers, "Sh-h-h. . . Just slip the candy into my top drawer"?

Following what seems to me like a short visit, Tim looks a little out of breath, so I start to leave. He reminds me to sign his "daily visitors" book, and mine is, quite untypically, the first signature of the day.

"See ya, Tim! Have a great evening!"

"See ya," he replies. Then he tells me, a freckle-faced, aging friend, that I am beautiful. I've heard him say that to a lot of other ladies at the nursing home, young and old alike, too. I want to give him another medal of appreciation for his collection, but a smile will have to do. He seems pleased with that as he reaches for the TV remote, and the sports channel comes on as I leave the room.

****

During a later visit, my friend shared with me that he didn't have long to live. He was right. His time—as is ours—was short.

I picture Coach Reed guiding Tim's first steps from the wheelchair into the expanse of heaven. And I envision Tim looking down to earth and smiling as he sees the many loving fans that he, himself, acquired along the way.

I'd Make a Poor Hunter

I ruthlessly trapped a mouse last night,

Methodically planned his demise—

A rodent murder, first degree;

I marked him with cunning as he peeked out at me.

A savage trap, forged with merciless vigor,

Capriciously snapped as he nosed toward the trigger.

Bait in his jaws, head locked secure,

Stretched out in shock, the mouse did not stir.

Mission concluded, the weapon was cleaned;

The mouse was disposed of, no evidence seen.

Awake through the evening, I felt ill at ease

That such a dastardly deed could have surfaced in me.

IT COULD HAVE BEEN ME

It could've been me.

I could be the one with strong arms and legs,

Ears that hear, eyes that see,

A mind that reads right, knows numbers, the ABCs.

Yep, it could've been me.

It could've been you.

You could be the one whose body doesn't move the same,

See the same, hear the same, learn the same

As other people do.

Yep, it could've been you.

But Mom and Dad see

Good things in me,

And the Lord loves me

As He loves you.

Someday in heaven

I'll be put together just right.

But for now, in my need,

I depend on you.

On the Rebound

Pick yourself up; shake the dust off your shoes!

Others have made it, and you can, too!

But remember that bitter taste of the earth

Just enough for compassion when a brother feels hurt.

Too often we hoard only good that we've tasted.

Wise lessons gained from the bad go wasted.

As you rise up, your discoveries might spare

Another man stumbling over your same, hard-learned error.

GIVE US THIS DAY

Every morsel of life

Is savory to the taste.

Even the crust I chew slowly, thoughtfully,

Knowing that goodness lies somewhere within.

Small Town...
Past "50"

WHO STOLE MY FACE?

Who stole my face?
(I think I know.)
She's surely a callous
And sneaky foe!

She left me with wrinkles;
Took my youthful skin;
Snatched my feminine cheekbones
And put hair on my chin!

My dimples are gone;
Now I've age spots galore.
On my forehead are valleys
That weren't there before!

Who is the culprit?
Is this just a sick joke?
The bags 'neath my eyes
Make me look like I've croaked!

There's a thief on the loose,
Getting by with this crime.
Somebody, nab her!
Her name is "Time!"

TRANSFORMATION

(Middle-age Spread and Other Alarming Features)

Amazing! Annoying! It happens so fast,

The feared transformation;

No mercy! No pass!

Mirrors are pitiless,

Showing wrinkles en masse.

Out pops a spider vein;

Oh, no! I have gas!

Cellulite covers my thighs, once so thin,

And from where I had one,

Hangs a new DOUBLE chin.

My "hourglass figure,"

A thing of the past,

Is covered with bulges,

And my backside is vast!

Plenty of eyes used to wink and admire;

Now they cast stares,

Having lost all desire.

Though my midsection's grown,

What's a pound, even two,

Since my husband's grown bald

And sports a potbelly, too?

Sleepless Nights

AGING HORMONES MEET WRITER'S BLOCK

Sleepless nights

The need to write

Refuses to let go

Jumbled words

Wandering thoughts

That will not gel

Become my foe

They won't line up

Or march to a beat

But prod and poke me instead

Stealing my peace

While they're incomplete

They ruthlessly frustrate

My need for sleep

Lighten Up!

Alone in the corner
Stands my exercise bike.
Workouts are good—
They're just not what I like.

Sweating the weight off
Sounds unappealing to me.
Pedaling nowhere
Ain't my cup o' tea.

I'd rather take walks,
But there's crime in the streets,
And though my doctor says, "Diet!"
That's no easy feat.

Still, I restrict my consumption,
As my physician's decreed;
I scratch off of my menu
The carrots and peas.

I've limited food
To ice cream and cake;
Only a dish full,
And only five times a day.

To wash it all down,
Just a milkshake or two,
A sacrifice surely
Since I'm used to a few.

Then after the long
And arduous task
Of watching my intake,
The day comes at last!

It's time to be weighed
After all the travail,
But when the nurse sees the numbers,
Her face becomes pale!

Despite all the abstaining
And calorie counts,
The scale caves in
Before I can dismount!

It just doesn't make sense;
Lord knows I've tried.
Do you think that the scale
Could have possibly lied?

AFTER "59"

Clock strikes twelve

another day

ends

middle age gone

"60" begins

Small Town...

Retirement

ABBY'S PRETTY TOENAILS

When my husband, in his retirement,

Is bored with nothing to do,

He paints our dog's long toenails

With sparkly pinks and blues.

There's glitter in the polish

To draw attention to her feet,

And people surely notice

When I walk Abby down the street.

How embarrassed I am as I pass by

Owners of leashed pedigrees.

They snicker; they snoot, and they shake their head—

Not the owners, it's their dogs, I mean!

A Boat Afloat After Winter

It skipped over waves on Lake Erie
On its maiden voyage of the year;
As the frost disappeared in April,
Out came the fishing gear.

The goal was to catch the limit
Of walleye or perch or both,
But half the fun was being out in the sun
For the old fisherman and his boat.

Along My Morning Path

Tall blades of grass wave and shimmer along my morning path. Glistening streams of sunlight peek through leafy branches, to bounce playfully off my walking shoes. Birds twitter happily, while a distant train whistles and moans in intervals as it carries its load responsibly down long, iron rails.

A Harley sputters by, strange accompaniment to wind chimes ringing daintily from fishing families' abodes. Filled with awesome wonder, I stroll back to Fenwick's campground and approach our modest trailer on the lake.

Years of work are now followed by some rest. Retirement is worthy of the wait.

Our A.D. Dixie Dog

As a retired teacher, I could spot the characteristics of attention deficit. But when I pointed out to my husband that our silver lab, Dixie, was "A.D," and undoubtedly hyperactive, too, my hubby flashed me a sarcastic grin, followed by, "She's still a pup."

"She's a year and a half now, Dear," I replied, "and there's no sign of her slowing down. It's hard to keep her attention, to get her to listen."

This was a canine that switched gears and lost touch with reality in an instant. Unless we carried a rolled-up newspaper with us at all times, Dixie paid no mind to consequences. She thrived on moment-to-moment excitement, fast-pacing from one thing to another, especially when she was bored.

We lost two sets of Venetian blinds on our patio doors as a result of Dixie's attempts to reach squirrels in our back yard. Another of her "antics" was chasing her tail, not just a few times, but 10-12 times until she ran into walls and furniture, and then she continued to circle the other way around. When she spotted a buzzing fly, she'd take off leaping from one end of the room to the other, trying to chomp the bug in mid-air. (There were many times I rushed behind her to catch lamps and breakables before they fell to the floor. . . Frustrating!)

Bedroom and bathroom doors had to be shut when Dixie was around. If not, the dog would leave a path of toppled waste cans, shredded toilet paper and tissues, and ravaged pillows in her wake. If I forgot to shut the bathroom door completely while styling my hair at the sink, the dog pushed the door open and barged in. Rising on her back paws, she'd snarl, growl, bark, and attack the hair dryer. I had to physically shove her out the door and lock it to avoid repeated intrusions.

One day, when we had neglected Dixie for only a matter of minutes, she became uncharacteristically quiet. Suspicious of her silence, I peeked around the corner into our family room to see what the dog was up to. Feathers hung from her muzzle and a turkey wing lay beneath her paws. She had jumped onto the couch in our family room and reached up to

pull Paul's prized, stuffed turkey mount from off the wall! "Oh, you've really done it this time!!!" I said. Dixie cowered and crawled toward her kennel. She opened the kennel door with her paw and went inside for "time out." To her credit, after Paul saw what she had done, Dixie learned to never bother his turkey trophies again!

When Dixie didn't get our exclusive attention, she sought acknowledgement in another, unusual way. My husband told me a couple times about something he caught her doing, but I found it hard to believe until I witnessed it myself. As I worked in the kitchen, I could see clearly over the countertop bar into the family room. Amazed, I watched Dixie crawl up on the arm of the couch next to the home phone unit, look up to see if I was observing, and then proceed to press the message recorder button with her paw and her nose! She rested next to the phone until all the messages had played! It was incredible!

I finally figured out that Dixie was not really attention deficit, as I originally thought. She acted out when she felt attention "deprived." Our dog Dixie craved constant human attention, and she sure knew how to get it!

Small Town...
Profound

HER CONTRIBUTION TO A CANDIDATE

Gracious but bold, intelligent, wise,

Her aged, bending body a misleading disguise;

'Neath curled, snowy locks, angelic array,

The old woman's Truth chases Darkness away.

Firm in conviction, she reassumes post;

Sits at her desk, this humanitarian host.

Quivering fingers locate the keys;

Her letter addresses our country's needs.

"God's been abandoned; Man turns his head;

Where neighbor helped neighbor, apathy treads.

All the drugs, corruption, and depravity

Can be beat if we call on the Authority.

"I've asked God's forgiveness for our nation's neglect,

Like irresponsible increase to trillions in debt;

I've pictured His tears as we abort His babies

And as we abuse born children and make objects of ladies.

"With all God's advice to us having been said

In His Word, meant to help us—providing it's read,

My campaign donation for meeting your goal

Is a prayer for revival of America's soul."

The letter was printed, signed and sealed;

Mailed to the site of the campaign appeal.

The prayer ended up, through the Lord's intervention,

On the winning candidate's wall, in the governor's mansion.

UNTITLED

He drugged himself to death;

Left a teenage son

Standing next to his casket

With no daddy,

No good memories.

Just a dead man

Lying pale and cold

In a wooden box

With a stiff arm that has a hole in it

Where the needle went in

When he drugged himself

To death.

SHE DIED ON HER BIRTHDAY

She took her last breath

when it had begun

on March 22nd

at age 81.

But during those years,

the ones in-between,

she danced and she whistled

and she dreamed.

She sang in the bathtub.

She skipped to her school.

She tended her flowers

and splashed in the pool.

She found the Lord Jesus

in the woods one day.

She read good books

and won a role in a play.

She married her sweetheart,

a hardworking boy;

There was romance and children

and joy.

She didn't die wealthy;

she gave it away

to others in need

after bills were paid.

She's missed by so many

but has left behind

a legacy of loving,

of touched hearts, and changed

lives.

Her ultimate gift,

Left for all to embrace—

is because she lived,

the world's a better place.

Seeing Haiti from on Top

Panoramic, mountaintop views.

Cement-block huts bearing rough-hewn doors and roofs of warped, rusty tin.

Churchgoers neatly dressed, proudly parading in their Sunday,

    second-hand best, wearing their only pair of shoes.

Children standing naked on the dry dirt road.

Visitors' havens offering clean showers gushing cool sprays of water

    from chrome faucets to waken Caucasian faces on a tropical morn.

Gourdeless pockets, bare breasts, bloated bellies, parched lips, thirsty tongues.

"Dolla, Sir?" asks a small black hand, outstretched, caked with dust.

I decline

As I buy one last souvenir to remember my trip to

Haiti.

*THIS FOLLOWS 3 SHORT MISSION TRIPS TO HAITI, WHERE HANDING OUT TREATS/MONEY CAN CAUSE HUMAN STAMPEDES.

LUNCH WITH AUNT ALVIRA

My 93-year-old aunt slowly, carefully, coaxes the corn from her plate onto her spoon. Then with a frail, trembling, but determined hand, she lifts the food to her lips, losing a few kernels along the way. "I'm so messy," she says in a raspy voice, and following a pause and the hint of a giggle, she adds, "I just dropped some corn on the floor." I swallow a bite from my own sandwich and offer to help her with hers, but she sweetly declines. Then after reconsideration, she invites me to cut her sandwich in half, if I would be so kind, she says. I am reminded of a time when dear Aunt Alvira was the helper who nursed and spoon-fed her 12 children, my cousins; the same nurturing lady who bottle-fed calves in the barn and spread grain for baby "peeps" in the chicken house.

"Would you like me to get a cookie for you?" I ask, thinking I might walk to the dessert counter to purchase some sweets to follow our meal, but Aunt Alvira tells me she has her daughter Sharon's fresh-baked oatmeal cookies on the dresser in her room. "Go and get. . . one for each of us. . . out of the jar," she says, clearing her throat a couple times before the sentence is complete. I comply.

Close to the cookie jar sits a 25th anniversary photograph of my aunt and her husband Harold, now gone many years. There's another photo taken with their children, another of their 47 grandchildren, and yet another set of photos show smiling samples of the 96 great-grandchildren. I refocus on the cookie jar, though, and after extracting two of the oatmeal delights, I return to my aunt, who is sitting patiently, peacefully, and unmoved in her wheelchair at the Oakridge Section #1 dining area table as if I never left.

I seat myself next to her again, and as we munch our cookies, Alvira sips her hot chocolate and I sip my coffee. Conversation resumes, this time about our very favorite desserts. I know what she is thinking before she even speaks it—pumpkin pie! Oh, how my auntie loves pumpkin pie! I look on the menu for supper, hoping, but her favorite is not on today's list. Then I walk down the aisle to the dessert counter, where I'm told it's not being carried either. "Maybe next month," the cashier says, and I think, *Who knows if we have next month, or even a tomorrow, especially if we're 93?*

After slight disappointment with the pumpkin pie outcome, the conversation remains on the general topic of food, but skips from desserts to recipes to fresh fruits and vegetables and then to the huge family garden Alvira used to tend from spring to fall. I remember when she raised her own corn, tomatoes, potatoes, green beans, cabbage, peas, beets, and melons, with a grape arbor on one side of the garden and the field where her husband worked the dirt on a tractor, on another side. Together, with all the kids helping, Harold and Alvira ran an efficient and healthy family operation. Most of the food on their table was home-grown and home-canned in quart jars to nourish the family through winter. There

were apple trees and strawberry patches for pies and jams in the summer, and home-raised beef, pork, and chicken all year long.

Our next topics at the lunch table are family weddings, relatives' health, and my aunt's great-grandbabies. Until a year or two ago, Aunt Alvira knew the name of every grandchild and great-grandchild. Today she feels bad, she says, that she's having a hard time remembering a few of the 143. "My mind must be slipping," she says with a twist of humor. I laugh, recalling how I occasionally call one of my sons by the other son's name, and my husband and I only have 3 children and 5 grandchildren's names to remember.

Our conversation switches from current, back to the past again, and we reminisce out loud. I remember vividly how, years ago, Aunt Alvira's family always made room for one more at their long table when I, or other cousins, came to visit for days at a time on their farm. There was the ritual of the silly "bean song" that Uncle Harold sang at the table every time visitors ate a meal with them. *Beans, beans, the musical fruit; the more you eat, the more you toot. The more you toot, the better you feel, so let's have beans at every meal!* The "bean song" only occurred after Harold led family prayer, of course, asking God to bless the food.

I remember, too, that Aunt Alvira and Uncle Harold's household was very organized, with daily chores marked next to names on the chalkboard. Out of fairness, responsibilities would be switched around occasionally, and visiting cousins were expected to participate in the work. We girls were usually the ones to sweep the kitchen floor, diaper the babies, help prepare the food, and do the dishes—using water that gushed from the hand pump built into the side of the long, porcelain sink. The cold water from the hand pump needed to be heated in a large tea kettle on the stove before we could use it to "suds up" for washing dishes and pots n' pans. Barnyard feeding, manure clean-ups, "slopping the hogs," and other outside work was usually left to the four boys in the family. Their eight sisters and I would finish chores first since we had a lot more helpers. We had a good time talking—and sometimes sang crazy songs—in the meantime. There sure was fun to be had for us all outside, though, if the chores of the day were completed before sundown, which was almost always the case in summer.

As Alvira and I continue, deep in our reminiscing, memories come up that make Auntie chuckle, like of their 2-holer "outhouse," the last one still in use for miles around, that could give the user frostbite in the dead of winter if you weren't "efficient." There were the baseball games in the barnyard, eating apples right off the trees, playing croquet and hoping you'd get picked for Cousin Doris's team or else you'd get beaten every time. There was swimming in the pond, past the lily pads and cumbersome moss. There was walking

through the spooky woods. . . and, of course, there were always homemade cookies galore! There was popcorn and Kool-Aid at night during the one hour allotted for TV before bedtime. And there was so much more. The memories connected to this wonderful family go on and on. While they couldn't afford to go on vacations, themselves, with their 12 kids, did Alvira and Harold realize they were hosting the best of summer vacations for others? The sharing of work, mealtime, and playtime built strong extended family relationships, too. Aunt Alvira and Uncle Harold's kids were like brothers and sisters to me, the siblings I never had, and some of us remain close to this day.

I suddenly feel compelled to say something to Alvira that's been building in my heart for a long time, and I can't keep it inside any longer. "Auntie, your family provided me, and the other cousins, with some of the happiest memories of our lives. As busy as you always were, you welcomed us to spend vacations with you on your farm in the summertime. You taught me what it means to put "work before play" but then to appreciate the fun part to the fullest; you showed me nurturing—of children, of animals, of plants in the garden; you taught me joy in togetherness. Thank you, Aunt Alvira," I tell her from the depth of my heart.

With a quaint smile and a slight nod of her head, she acknowledges what I have said, and without any words of her own, sends a "heart hug" from across the table. Though her eyes and legs and hands are failing her, her love and wisdom are not.

I look up at the clock and see that time has passed by quickly. That is confirmed, in another sense, as I notice my auntie's veined, wrinkled hands hanging over the armrest of her wheelchair and as I, each morning, witness tissue-paper skin developing on my own hands, and lines appearing on my own face. "Laugh lines" I call them jokingly, but I know better. The aging phenomenon that used to transform "other" people is now getting closer to home. Ties between past and present become more meaningful. Time becomes more precious; what we do with it becomes more significant, and there is a sense of urgency that youth cannot grasp but that becomes realized with age.

"Good-bye, Aunt Alvira. I'll see you next week!" – As I get up from my chair, I hope that it is true.

ALVIRA C. KAISER, BORN OCTOBER 15, 1920
DIED MARCH 29, 2017

THE SEAGULL

Atop the pole the seagull reigns,
Self-absorbed and self-proclaimed,
Higher Power it disdains,
As it squawks in its feathered finery.

Until a wisp of wind blows by,
Toppling the bird down from the sky.
Once perched above, it lived, it died,
An arrogant fatality.

At the Nursing Home

The first time I saw them

He was nudging her wheelchair

Down the hallway

An inch at a time

As he scooted behind her in his own.

I remember thinking,

"This is love."

But I was wrong.

It came later.

The old man leaned forward,

Smoothed his sweetheart's white hair

And whispered her name.

His wife of five decades turned to ask,

"Who are you?"

"I'm Henry," he said sweetly,

And he caressed her hand.

Then they continued,

Two wheelchairs

Down a long hallway,

The woman

And the man.

Small Town... *Faith*

THIS EARTHLY LIFE

This Life

What a ride!

Exhilarating!

Ups

Downs

Boosts

Bumps

Look over your shoulder

To see what's past—

Gone.

Look ahead

To all that is left

Blessings

Regrets

Family

Faith

Friends

The

End. . .

Pause

Then. . .

Needle in a Haystack?

(How about a Contact Lens in a Lawn?)

About 75 Kaisers had clustered around my grandparents' willow tree during the family reunion picnic, when a cry of panic cut through the scene of celebration. My hands flew up to my mouth, gaped in shock, and I realized the cry had come from me. Suddenly, the sight in my left eye had become ominously blurred. My footsteps halted, and I dropped down to my knees when I realized what had happened. My lens had popped out. Somewhere below me, or around me, in the vast stretch of lush, spring-green grass, lay hidden my plastic, GREEN contact lens, and its whereabouts seemed impossible to detect. The old saying played across my mind like words rolling across a marquee . . . How do you find a needle in a haystack?

"You might as well plan on wearing your glasses until you can get a replacement," said my Uncle Bud. The other relatives agreed and went on with the picnic—except for one.

"Don't give up hope, my dear. Miracles happen. You will see. We'll search the area that you walked," my always hopeful Aunt Marie encouraged me. I appreciated her attempt at consolation and agreed to her suggestion of a search, though inside, I dismissed her optimism with a reality check.

Fifteen minutes or more passed by as my aunt and I combed through the grass looking for the missing contact lens. I held my hand over my left eye all the while as I tried to focus as best I could with my right. *How ridiculous this must appear to the others*, I thought, as my aunt and I searched the lawn. We moved on our knees like snails, and in our short pants and sneakers, we reaped nothing but grass stains during our hunt. I was becoming increasingly despondent when I heard a sudden gasp.

"What's wrong?" I asked my father's sister, feeling the time had come to call off the search.

Aunt Marie had fixed her eyes on a tiny glint of light peeking through the grass. She pointed in its direction. She insisted, "Honey, come over here!"

There, in a thick patch of green, lay my equally green contact lens. It glowed in the light of a single sunbeam, between the blades of grass! The only thing that shone brighter than the sun that afternoon was the smile on my aunt's face following the improbable discovery. My mouth gaped in amazement as I carefully, methodically picked up the lens and cupped it in my hand. "This can't be real," I said. Relatives congregated around me, gazing in disbelief.

For some time afterwards, Aunt Marie and I pondered the odds of such an outcome. Her faith had kept me going, or I would have given up. And I've fancied a thought or two about that light that shone on my lens. I just wonder. . . Many years ago, another search went on, and the seekers found their prize at the end of another beam of light. It directed three wise men to a discovery of much more monumental significance than my own. . . Could that beam of light and my beam of light have come from the same source? I wonder. I like to think it did.

WHEN YOU THOUGHT NO ONE WAS WATCHING
(...HE WAS)

Today my very well-being
Totally depends on you.
But someday in God's glorious Kingdom
My body and mind will be new.

Then I'll be watching a rerun
Of the kindness you've always shown,
Like the pats on the head and shoulder
When you thought we were here alone.

I'll be sitting right next to Jesus
To explain all you did for me
When you thought no one was watching,
But there will be nothing He's not already seen.

We'll watch the whole playback together—
Your sweetness when some might be mad,
And when you squeezed my hand to assure me
That things were not so bad.

Your voice was calm and soothing.
When I was hurting, you came to my aid;
Your presence was all I needed.
Jesus saw the difference you made.

Someday soon I'll thank you
For all that you do today.
When you come knocking on heaven's door,
I'll ask Jesus to let you stay.

The Most Glorious Sight
(Revelation at the Gas Pump)

It was the most glorious sight! I seriously thought the Lord was returning for His people, and though I'd pondered it often, I was surprised at my own reaction. I was ready and excited to go! Who would have ever thought such a spectacular, unforgettable moment would happen while at a gas station, mundanely pumping fuel into your car?

I was returning from several days of cleaning and writing at our family trailer on Lake Erie. My gas gauge showed almost "empty," so I stopped to fill up. As I glanced back and forth from the increasing dollar amount on the pump to the handle gushing gas into my Pontiac Vibe, I looked up to the sky for a moment. It seemed peculiar. A straight line across the heavens split the ominous, dark, rolling clouds of the southern half from the bright, cheerful sky of the northern half. I thought, *Looks like a bad storm, either coming or going. I hope it passes. We could be in for a lot of rain.*

Then, my focus shifted from the south to the northwestern sky, and, oh! It was breathtaking! The sun was a living, white, misty orb, surrounded by a mystical aura. As I stood overwhelmed by the sight, I suddenly felt a peace that I had never experienced before— and total, inexpressible joy! *Is this what heaven is like?* I wondered, and I didn't want to move. I wanted to stay in the moment forever.

When I finally went inside the gas station to pay my bill, the cashier looked at me strangely. *Does heaven show on my face?* I asked myself. Then the words were gushing out of me uncontrollably. I told her about the vibrant, white sun, and the line separating the darkness from the light, and the. . . But then I stopped. She looked at me like I was crazy.

That day's experience, or shall I say "revelation," will stay with me until I take my last breath. If it's true that our time on this earth is just a pebble on the beach of eternity, the "forever-joy" of heaven is simply unfathomable.

PUTTING GOD IN LINE

We remember God's Love, but forget He is just,

And as we busily attend to our needs,

We put Him in line to wait His turn

After Facebook, football, and cable TV.

Could the day come that we stand in a line

Waiting to enter the door,

When God steps out, stares and asks,

"Who are you? Have I met you before?"

SHOWING RESPECTS

I walked with 3-year-old Eva and her daddy, our son Dan, across the cemetery to "show respects" at my parents' grave on Memorial Day weekend 2018. One at a time I snipped the silk flowers, handed them to Dan and Eva, who arranged them in the tombstone vases. It was a learning opportunity for my granddaughter, and I prayed that the right words would come into my mind and my heart.

"This is what we call 'showing respects,' Eva. I loved my mom and dad, your Great-Grandma Helen and your Great-Grandpa Paul, and I visit their gravesite once in a while. Here I remember good things about our life together before they died. Someday, you'll be able to show your respects to Grandpa and me and bring us flowers, too."

Realizing that in recent months I had told Eva in simple, child-like terms, about heaven (up above) and hell (down below the ground) when we read children's Bible books, I knew I had to choose my words carefully when I explained burial to her.

"When we die, though our bodies are buried in the ground, that's not the same as going to the bad place in hell. We're talking two different things. And remember that if we have loved the Lord, our hearts (our souls) go up to heaven to be happy with Him forever." As Eva looked at the engravings on the tombstone, the thoughts seemed to be sinking in.

Pointing to a huge statue about 20 yards from where we stood, she said, "Grandma, I want to take a walk over there to see the big Jesus."

Then this pretty little girl in the flowery yellow dress and I, her grandma, limping with a cane, took the path together to rest our thoughts at the foot of the cross.

Scanning the expanse of hundreds of tombstones that lay before us, I was given a glimpse of life's continuum. Four generations of my family were here: my parents, myself, my son, and my granddaughter. It wasn't just the bloodline that tied us together. It was memories. It was the promise of life after this one. And it was love.

THE BIG PICTURE

The Big Picture escapes us.

We lose sleep and trouble our souls

Over trivial things

That matter not in the course of time;

While the Almighty,

The Purpose,

The Sole Provider,

Beckons every single day.

We rush to read the daily news,

But pass up

The Eternal Living Word.

Awaken My Senses

Awaken all my senses, Lord,
To Your blessings from above
So every day I marvel at
The wonders of Your love.

Take these worldly blinders off
My eyes so I can see
That every day's a miracle
That Your life bought for me.

That blue cathedral ceiling;
The rays of shining light
That sparkle on the ocean;
The stars that fill the night—

They're the message of Your greatness
Just outside my door.
I only need to look around
For a glimpse of what's in store.

Though I can't be but a petal
In the orchard of Your love;
Still, look at all You've given me
From Your treasure chest above!

I'm so undeserving
Of a God so great as You,
Who sacrificed His life for me,
To make my life brand new.

You're the God of miracles,
The generous "I AM,"
The Lord of all Creation,
The gentle, loving Lamb!

Help me to appreciate
The gifts that I ignore;
A million daily miracles
Right outside my door.

ABOUT THE AUTHOR

Judy Bruns holds a Bachelor's degree in education and a Masters degree in guidance counseling. She has taught grammar and literature classes, creative writing, and coached Power of the Pen teams in Ohio schools. She is a wife, a mother, a grandmother, and an ardent volunteer for causes close to her heart. Besides *Rhymes & Ramblings of a Small Town Girl*, Bruns has written 8 children's picture books, a book for teachers on "story"/narrative writing, and numerous articles that have appeared in newspapers and magazines.

Other Books by Judy Bruns:
Prompts That Make Kids BEG To Write!
    (200 middle school prompts)

Children's picture books:
Donnie, Lost in the Cornfield
Hattie and Her 43 Cats
Now I'm a BIG Girl
Now I'm a BIG Boy
Billy Joe Boomershine and the Toilet Paper Bandit
Painting Grandma's Nails
Thousand Dollar Baseball
Quilt Us a Rock! (newest release)